FOREWORD

Flipside incorporates three traditional tales into one full-length performance. Three stories passed down through the ages - they depict different times and different cultures but essential themes remain unchanged. Who, among so many characters, can see the truth and act upon it? In two tales from Eastern Europe and one from Ancient Persia, feisty characters cut through shallow concerns to demonstrate what really matters. Orphan Evichka in *The Twelve Stones* has to do the bidding of her outrageously evil stepmother and stepsister – but where will their demands lead them? One of Shakespeare's sources for *King Lear*, the youngest daughter in Czech story *Salt is Sweeter than Gold* refuses to be like her sisters, and speaks truthfully to her father instead of flattering him, despite the consequences. As for Nasrudin, a folk-hero celebrated by many continents and cultures from the Middle East to Central Asia, is he wise man or fool?

Devised to appeal to multi-aged, family audiences, *Flipside* is suitable for performance by Key Stages 3 and 4 and top juniors, for whole-school and youth theatre productions. Individual stories or scenes can also be used for text-based and improvisation work for drama lessons or youth theatre sessions.

The trilogy has been dramatised to allow great flexibility in cast size. Well-suited to an ensemble performance style, the tales offer plenty of on-stage opportunity for all participants. Extensive use of narrators allows equal sharing of lines in addition to character roles.

The performers are required to suggest place and environment physically, also enabling dance groups to be involved if available. A number of scenes have directions for improvisation to allow imaginative development of text, both in drama lessons and for performance.

CAST LIST

BARD 1
BARD 2
NARRATORS: 7, although number can expand or contract according to cast size

THE TWELVE STONES: A TRADITIONAL EASTERN-EUROPEAN TALE

EVICHKA
STEPMOTHER
STEPSISTER

STONES:
MAN WINTER
SPRING
SUMMER
AUTUMN
EIGHT NON-SPEAKING STONES

FIRE DANCERS

SALT IS SWEETER THAN GOLD: A TRADITIONAL CZECH TALE

BABICHKA
YOUNG WOMAN 1
YOUNG WOMAN 2

COURT:
KING
SISTER 1: The king's daughter

SISTER 2: The king's daughter
SALT PRINCESS: The king's youngest daughter
COOK
GUARD 1
GUARD 2
COURTIER 1
COURTIER 2
PHYSICIAN
NOBLE 1
NOBLE 2
4 MESSENGERS
DOORMAN
CROWD LEADER

NASRUDIN'S COAT: AN ANCIENT PERSIAN TALE

NASRUDIN
SERVANT
AUNT
14 GUESTS: Number can expand/contract according to cast size
TAILOR

Flipside includes many non-speaking roles/tableaux which can be played/formed by existing members of the cast.

With roles doubled it is possible to perform with a minimum of 15 (or fewer for individual stories). However, for a large-scale production, it accommodates a huge number of participants – particularly when different casts are used for each story. Set requirements are minimal in order to maintain fast pace and seamless transition between scenes. Suggestions for props and costumes are included at the end.

THE TWELVE STONES: A
TRADITIONAL EASTERN-EUROPEAN TALE

Scene 1

Cast (except Evichka, Stepmother and Stepsister) enter, warming up on stage. They move about silently while getting into position. Fire dancers in a group, centre back, and stones/narrators form semi-circle either side of fire dancers to frame action when not involved. Bards 1 and 2 enter together, address audience directly.

BARD 1:   *[Points to cast, sarcastic]* Apparently, it's all the rage

BARD 2:   to prance and sing upon the stage.

Cast begin softly chanting 'Ah-m' sound

BARD 1:   *[Points to audience]* You have come and paid your due.

BARD 2:   Your cash, a hook to catch the new.

BARD 1:   Yet all we offer: three tales of old

BARD 2:   filled with lads and lasses bold.

Cast adopt caricature-like postures to simulate lads/lasses bold

BOTH: Hmmm…

BARD 1:   But wait, before you grind your teeth,

BARD 2:   we beg you first, let disbelief

BARD 1:   be carried off by every tale.

BARD 1:   By evening's end, we will not fail

BARD 2:   to make you pause and maybe savour

BARD 1:   imagination's dark, rich flavour.

Evichka enters. Stands centre-stage. Cast adopt tableaux at rear of stage

BARD 1:   So, here's a girl whose smile, once bright,

BARD 2:   now dimmed by working through the night,

BARD 1:   is made to do the menial chores,

BARD 2:   without affection or applause.

BARD 1:   A tale with echoes of another

BARD 2:   and an unexpected sort of godmother.

BARD 1:   Sit back, get comfy, enjoy the ride.

BARD 2:   This coin gets a new

BOTH: flipside!

Cast have continued to quietly chant 'Ah-m' under bards' speech. When bards finish speaking, the chant changes from 'Ah-m' to 'Stone', repeated and lengthened in sound. Bards allow sound to build then cut it, making slicing movement with hands. Sound stops. Bards exit. Stepmother and Stepsister enter. All whisper the title 'The Twelve Stones,' then make cold sounds – windy, whistling and shushing sounds – as narrators begin speaking. Sounds stop as Narrator 7 finishes speaking. Evichka and Stepmother and Stepsister mime the activities described

NARRATOR 1: In long ago days, a young woman called Evichka lived in a small stone cottage with her stepsister and stepmother.

NARRATOR 2: She was made to do all the work about the house:

NARRATOR 3: from the cooking

NARRATOR 4: to the washing

NARRATOR 5: to the sweeping of the cold stone floors.

NARRATOR 6: There should be laws against that! Even worse, her stepsister and stepmother sat idly around.

NARRATOR 7: Typical!

NARRATOR 6: It was the middle of a long, cold winter, and Evichka had just got the fire going in the grate.

Fire dancers can create image of fire flaring up

Scene 2

Improvised scene with Evichka, Stepmother and Stepsister. Stepmother is idle and bored. She has sudden idea that 'Some purple violet flowers would so brighten this dull room.' She immediately orders Evichka to find some: 'And never mind that it's the middle of winter.' Stepsister whines and preens alongside her mother. She also bosses Evichka around in highly insulting manner.

Stepmother and Stepsister should be as stereotypically nasty as possible to create humorous baddies. Evichka is unfalteringly polite and subservient. She is resigned to her role and never attempts to answer back. Evichka has no choice other than to do as she's told. She moves to the side to put on a thin, moth-eaten cloak and picks up her basket. Exit Stepmother and Stepsister.

Scene 3

Cast make cold sounds. Continue until Narrator 2 stops speaking.
Evichka mimes actions described.

NARRATOR 1: Out she went into the cold, with only a thin
cotton cloak against the wind.

EVICHKA: How shall I find purple violets in winter?

Cast switch from cold sounds to repeated, whispered echo of 'How?
Violets? Winter? How? Violets? Winter? How? Violets? Winter?' As
they speak, cast move into position to represent a forest. Resume
cold sounds

NARRATOR 2: The cold beat into her and she lost her way.

Evichka mimes getting tangled up in the forest of arms barring her
way. She emerges at the back of the stage and freezes as the cast
reform into a semi-circle of 12 stones with the fire dancers in tableau
in the centre. Stones face outwards

> She found herself at last at the top of a hill where a
> circle of twelve tall stones stood. In the middle of the
> circle a fire roared.

Fire dancers come to life

EVICHKA: *[Watches the fire from outside the circle for a moment,*
allowing dance to develop] Please forgive me if I
intrude but I would ask your permission to warm
myself awhile by this fire. *[She steps hesitantly and*
gently towards the fire dancers]

NARRATOR 3: As she crossed the circle, the stones changed into
twelve men of all different ages:

All stones turn inwards as she passes inside the circle

NARRATOR 4: some very old, some not so old and some ever so young. The oldest, with a white beard that flowed like a river, came towards her.

If using music for fire dance, fade out. Dancers form a mound, kneeling in an inward-facing circle, with heads bowed in centre

MAN WINTER: Why is your face so sad, little one?

EVICHKA: I have to find purple violets or my stepmother will beat me!

MAN WINTER: Banish fear, dear one, for we shall help you. Spring, my young comrade, step forward. Take your axe and use it to summon a moment from your heart.

SPRING: *[Takes axe and whirls it around head. Sings or speaks]*

Come, seeds sow,
Come, breeze blow,
Water flow
From our hearts
To the earth
Where flowers grow.

NARRATOR 5: And as that axe whirled, the air grew warmer, the grass looked greener and there! Purple violets began to push up from the ground.

Fire dancers each push one hand up through mound and then open hands to reveal cloth violets growing

EVICHKA: *[Gasps, then picks violets]* How can I ever thank you? I will forever remember the magic of this kindness. Farewell, with thanks. *[She steps out of the circle]* Surely now my stepmother will be happy; surely she will treat me well. Oh, surely...surely. *[Freezes]*

Cast repeat 'Surely, surely' as stones and fire dancers move aside. Stepmother and Stepsister enter, miming looking through window for Evichka's return. They spot her and she enters

STEPMOTHER: So you're back, hmmm? What kept you, eh? How dare you keep us waiting so long! *[She grabs the flowers]* Here, give them to me now.

STEPSISTER: What are you staring at?

STEPMOTHER: Insolent girl! Get to bed immediately, I can't bear to see your miserable face another moment. *[She thrusts basket back to Evichka]*

STEPSISTER: Me neither. Ugly, snivelling little wretch. And just be grateful we don't make you sleep in a kennel.

Evichka lies down at side of stage after putting cloak in basket

STEPSISTER: I say, Mummy, why do we let her sleep in the house? So unhygienic!

Stepmother sniffs violets then tosses them over her shoulder onto floor. Both freeze

NARRATOR 6: Cold and hungry, Evichka slept as the sweet scent of violets filled the house.

Cast breathe in and exhale as though smelling the flowers, then all droop as though sleeping

Scene 4

NARRATOR 7: The next morning, Evichka's stepmother tried to think of another great and rather cruel idea.

All stretch and wake, suddenly alert, except Evichka, who sleeps on

Improvised scene with Evichka, Stepmother and Stepsister. Stepmother is irritable, trying to settle on what to ask Evichka to find next. Stepsister suggests strawberries but is shushed by mother who is 'Trying to concentrate on thinking up a really clever idea.' Stepmother turns to reveal her own idea: strawberries! She bawls Evichka's name several times, wakes her roughly, demands strawberries, 'Who cares that it's the middle of winter?' and turns the girl outside with a grunt of satisfaction. As before, Stepsister joins in with the orders, sarcasm and demands.

Evichka grabs cloak and basket. Stepmother and Stepsister exit. Cast repeat sequence of moves from Scene 3 to create forest and get into stone circle formation.

NARRATOR 1: Out Evichka went into the cold, with only a thin cotton cloak against the wind.

EVICHKA: How shall I find wild strawberries in winter?

Cast whisper 'How? Strawberries? Winter? How? Strawberries? Winter?'

NARRATOR 2: A chilling rain soon soaked her and she could not find her way.

Cast use fingers to rain down on Evichka as she passes among trees. All repeat 'Pitter, patter' until stone circle forms

At last, she came upon the top of a hill where a circle of twelve tall stones stood. In the middle of the circle a fire danced.

Fire dancers dance

EVICHKA: Please forgive me if I intrude, but I would ask your permission to dry myself awhile by this fire. *[She moves to warm her hands]*

NARRATOR 3: As she crossed the circle, the stones suddenly turned into twelve men of all different ages, some ever so young, some not so young and some as old as dreams. The oldest, with a white beard that fell like a wave, came towards her.

Fire dancers repeat mound shape formation

MAN WINTER: Why is your face so sad, little one?

EVICHKA: I have to find wild strawberries or my stepmother shall beat me!

MAN WINTER: Learn hope, my dear, for we shall help. Summer, my golden, bright friend, step forward with your box of colours and your promise of light.

SUMMER: *[Takes out a box of coloured dust and sprinkles it in a wide arc as speaks or sings]*

Take these colours, air,
Take these colours, ground,
And mix a palette rare
Where summer fruits are found.

NARRATOR 4: As the box emptied, the air grew warm and the sun peered through the clouds. Where each speck of colour fell, a flower grew and sweet strawberries crept out of the soil.

Fire dancers each roll backwards simultaneously in a smooth, sinuous movement, holding cloth strawberries aloft in right hand. Like synchronised swimmers, the formation should resemble an open flower from which the strawberries have grown

EVICHKA: My thanks are too many all to be spoken and your kindness is warmer than the fire itself. And now, perhaps, Stepmother will be happy. *[She freezes]*

Cast whisper 'Happy, happy, happy.' They move back. Stepmother and Stepsister enter and move centre stage. Evichka arrives

STEPMOTHER: Have you got them? Have you? Well? Hmmm. *[Grabs strawberries and crams one in her mouth]* Mmmmm! Delicious! *[Turns accusingly to Evichka]* Clever! Too clever. Get out of my sight!

STEPSISTER: Yes! And stop breathing near me! I don't want to catch anything from you! *[Pushes Evichka then looks at her hands in horror and wipes them]*

STEPMOTHER: Oh, and as you took so long, we gave our supper leftovers –

STEPSISTER: Mummy means *your* supper, that is –

STEPMOTHER: to the dog. That ought to teach you to be a bit quicker next time.

STEPSISTER: Lazy little skiver! Oh, and we gave your bed to the dog too. You'll be on the floor from now on.

NARRATOR 5: Evichka huddled up without tasting a single red fruit.

Evichka huddles inside her cloak in a corner. Stepmother and Stepsister turn backs to audience and freeze

Scene 5

Evichka has hardly closed eyes when Stepmother shakes her awake.

NARRATOR 6: The next morning, Stepmother woke with a brilliant idea.

STEPMOTHER: Green apples! Out! Now! Who cares that it's winter? Come along. Off you go!

Laughs, points outside. Stepmother and Stepsister rub hands together. Evichka wearily picks up basket

STEPSISTER: You are SO smart and clever Mummy. What a simply super idea. The crunchy sharpness of apples – just perfect after the scrummy sweetness of those strawberries. Mmmmm.

Exit Stepmother and Stepsister

NARRATOR 7: Out Evichka had to go into the cold, with only the thinnest of cotton cloaks against the wind.

EVICHKA: How shall I find green apples in winter?

Cast whisper 'How? Apples? Winter? How? Apples? Winter?'

NARRATOR 1:The clouds weighed upon her and a mist turned her way into a maze of shadow.

Cast swirl around Evichka, chanting 'Mist, lost, mist, lost' then move into stone circle position

After a time, she found herself at the top of a hill where a circle of twelve stones stood. In the middle of the circle a fire sang.

Fire dancers form fire tableau but remain still, making vocal sounds of fire instead. Gradually fade to silence during next speech

NARRATOR 2: As she crossed the circle, the stones suddenly turned into twelve men of all different ages, some so young, some so old and some of middle-age. The oldest, with a white beard like feathers, came towards her.

MAN WINTER: Why is your face so sad, little one?

EVICHKA: I have to find green apples or my stepmother will beat me!

MAN WINTER: Autumn, my sad-eyed friend, please join us and lend us your song.

AUTUMN: *[Steps forward and sings or speaks]*
Fly, fly, fly,
The leaves are turning to gold,
Cold is the breeze,
Summer is waning.

Fire dancers switch position into tree tableau. Each dancer holds an apple in each hand as though suspended from a branch

NARRATOR 3: At the sound of his voice Evichka could have begun crying and never stopped.

Fire dancers begin swaying, as though in a wind

And so it was with the trees, which now had leaves like crowns, only to bow over in the wind and let them go like tears.

Evichka rushes around trees as apples are dropped into apron/basket

Into Evichka's apron fell many green apples. She found it hard to tear herself away.

EVICHKA: My heart is so full with your song and your gifts. I can only say thank you. It doesn't seem enough. Farewell... I'll hear your voice ever in my thoughts.

Evichka freezes. All stay in position. Cast repeat 'Ever' in a whisper as stones turn back to face outwards and fire dancers move aside. Stepmother and Stepsister enter and walk forward

STEPMOTHER: So where are they?

STEPSISTER: Give me one now! *[Stamps her foot]*

STEPMOTHER: What are you looking so dreamy about? Think you're clever do you? Do you? Get into that scullery!

STEPSISTER: There's plenty of washing up waiting – to keep idle hands busy.

STEPMOTHER: And plenty of icy water to draw from the well. I want it all done before midnight. You've been slacking in your duties, my girl.

Evichka turns, moves to rear of stage and sinks to knees. Stepmother and Stepsister fall on the apples hungrily then freeze in still tableau

NARRATOR 4: That night, Evichka slept hungry once more.

She slumps sideways, sleeping. Stones remain facing outwards

Scene 6

Improvised scene with Stepmother and Stepsister.

Stones remain in place. Stepmother and Stepsister come to life from their tableau and perform at front of stage. Stepsister thinks it odd that Evichka should find such fruit in winter. She wants to get some for herself as, after all, she's much more clever than Evichka. She decides to find where the tasty apples have come from. She's not worried about the winter cold – she has a fine warm coat. She's not interested in how she'll find apples, only where. Stepmother waves her off and exits.

Stepsister sets out, creeping along the front of the stage and around the stone circle. As she moves around, the fire dancers step back into tableau centre-stage in the middle of the stones.

NARRATOR 5: Soon, she found herself at the top of a hill where there stood a circle of twelve stones. In the middle, a fire beckoned to her.

Stepsister pushes through from the back, rudely and impatiently

NARRATOR 6: She pushed past the stones, not noticing them change into twelve men of twelve different ages until the oldest, with a beard that unfurled like fog, spoke.

Stepsister has her back to Man Winter as she warms her hands

MAN WINTER: How can I help you, my lady?

Stepsister jumps and turns round to face audience with back to fire

STEPSISTER: Who are you, ugly old man? I demand some apples, the same as my stupid sister found!

Man Winter steps back, smiling at the fire. Stepsister stamps her foot and continues to shriek. Fire dancers move closer behind her back, leaning towards her and fanning arms around her

I demand some apples! I deserve more than her! I demand what I deserve! Demand! Demand! Are you listening? I demand it!

Repeat to a scream as fire dancers burn around her

NARRATOR 7: And as her voice grew higher, so did the flames, until the fire leaned over to kiss her and she was... burned to... nothing.

Fire dancers pull her into their midst. She disappears behind the fire group. Dancers freeze, look up, smile and repeat in a whisper, 'Nothing.' Stones turn back to face outwards and freeze. The still-sleeping Evichka at rear of stage wakes and mimes domestic activity as Stepmother paces

> All this while, as Evichka cooked and washed, her stepmother paced up and down.

Stones and dancers remain in place. Stepmother grabs Evichka and throws her towards front of stage

STEPMOTHER: Where on earth can that daughter of mine be? I bet she's gobbling apples all by herself. Greedy lump! I'll show her. I'll find my own. After all, if you can do it anyone can. Who cares that it's winter. I have my fine, warm coat.

Evichka watches her go, then slumps down again at rear of stage with her back to audience

NARRATOR 1: Out she went, into the cold that was now deathly still. No bird sang, nor wind whispered and the mean woman could easily see the hill with the fire reaching into the sky from its top.

Stepmother creeps all the way around the circle (or moves through the audience). Fire dancers burn slowly

NARRATOR 2: She made her way up until she came to twelve tall stones that stood in a circle. These, she roughly pushed past to warm her hands by the fire.

Stones turn

NARRATOR 3: Never did she notice the stones change into men of all different ages, some young, some old and all without greed in their hearts. The oldest came towards her. He had a beard as white as dandelions and wild as the briar bush.

MAN WINTER: What would you have, my dear one?

STEPMOTHER: Your green apples, the ones that my stepdaughter found!

MAN WINTER: And are you willing to dance the dance of the seasons for them?

STEPMOTHER: I want the apples, so if such silliness is needed, then yes, stupid old man!

NARRATOR 4: With that, Spring stepped forward and swung his axe. As he did, grass began to grow between the fingers of the old woman, and out of her head.

Two dancers step forward and lace their fingers in between hers and over her head, from behind

NARRATOR 5: Then Summer stepped forward to sprinkle her with his box of colours. As the dust settled, flowers sprouted out of her nose, her ears and in her eyes.

Two more dancers form fists near her face, which sprout as the words are spoken

NARRATOR 6: She tried crying out, but Autumn stepped forward and simply sang. Then the woman did cry and cry and cry until all her body melted away, leaving only the cold, cold box of her heart.

Stepmother covers face and mimes crying. Dancers fold around her, shielding her so that she disappears. She places small box on the floor

MAN WINTER: Oh! You and I are so alike and it is a pity you could not see!

NARRATOR 7: Then he took her heart and cracked it in his icy hands.

Winter picks up the box and twists it in half

NARRATOR 1: Out of that box fell a flurry of snow that turned into a storm.

All on stage, including Stepmother, swirl around each other in a flurry of movement. Evichka swirls with them and lies down in the middle of the stage, asleep. Rest of cast twirl to the sides of the stage

Far below in the cottage, Evichka slept as the snow layered the land to pure white again.

NARRATOR 2: In the morning, the snow began to melt and birds sang, knowing that spring was on the way. Evichka woke feeling full of peace.

NARRATOR 3: And from that day on, her garden bore fruit in every season.

NARRATOR 4: And she never missed her stepsister or mother

NARRATOR 5: in

NARRATOR 6: the

NARRATOR 7: least.

Music. Cast exit. Bards walk to front of stage. Music fades

Scene 7

BARD 1:   Result! I really liked the bit about…

BARD 2:   When Stepmum's eyes had flowers popping out?

BOTH: Yeah!

BARD 1:   Sister in flames! Grisly *and* gory,

BARD 2:   hardly a happy-ever-after story!

BARD 1:   Except for the girl… no more chores.

BARD 2:   She gets the house, and our applause!

Both clap and indicate to audience to join in. Bards improvise shouted comments 'Bravo,' 'Hear, hear,' 'More,' 'You show 'em girl!' 'Bullies die!' 'Beats James Bond any day!' etc, building up until they are over-the-top with exaggerated praise. As audience stops clapping, Bard 1 notices audience again. They both fall into embarrassed silence

BARD 1: Err. Right. Where were we? You lot still here?

BARD 2: Perhaps they want their money's worth.

BARD 1: Oh dear.

BARD 2: Come on then. Second tale: might look like a repeat,

BARD 1: as if you've walked a familiar street

BARD 2: but here is yet another girl.

Salt Princess enters and pauses, frozen. Bard 2 breaks off and turns to Bard 1 in stage-whispered aside

Are you sure this is the right one?

BARD 1: Course I am, stupid.

BARD 2: Are you calling me stupid?

BARD 1: Do you see anyone else *stupid* round here, actually?

BARD 2: *[Sweeps arm round towards audience]* Yes... *actually!*

BARD 1: Point taken. *[Aside to audience]* Excuse my workmate! A few sentences short of a paragraph. What I have to put up with! *[Turns and hits Bard 2 over head with prop of choice]* As I was saying – but here is yet another girl *[Prods Bard 2 to get on with it]*

Salt Princess unfreezes and walks forward

BARD 2: whose life will soon be in a whirl.

Courtly music accompanies entrance of whole cast of Salt is Sweeter than Gold. They form court scene. Some are servants, standing by King. His three daughters, including the Salt Princess, take their places at the back, sewing. Courtiers 1 and 2 stand together in a corner. Babichka stands near the back. Others, including narrators, stand in groups around stage. Music fades.

Everyone looks bored while bards comment on tableau

BARD 1:   He's a king and father growing old,

BARD 2:   whose heart is filling up with cold.

Bards exit while muttering

BARD 1:   What is it with these parents in these plots?

BARD 2:   They need to get their *act* together.

BARD 1:   Oh. Dear. Was that supposed to be funny?

BARD 2:   I thought it was. A little theatrical… punning?

Court tableau is about to come to life. Narrator 1 draws breath and begins speaking but is rudely interrupted

NARRATOR 1: The king…

Bards rush back on stage

BARD 1:   Hang on a minute…

Cast looks at them very annoyed, calling out 'Call this professional?' 'My granny's handbag has more stage presence than you,' 'My gerbil is a better performer!' etc

BARD 1:   Really, *really* sorry about this.

BARD 2:   A vital point you cannot miss;

BARD 1:   in this tale that lies ahead,

BARD 2:   there is a custom of salt and bread.

BARD 1:   Tradition says it *must* be proffered,

BARD 2:   to every guest and visitor offered.

BARD 1:   So let the story *now* unfold

BARD 2:   where salt,

BARD 1:   my friends,

BARD 2:   is sweeter than gold.

Bards exit

SALT IS SWEETER THAN GOLD: A
TRADITIONAL CZECH TALE

Scene 8

Narrator 1 steps forward again. All whisper in unison 'Sweeter than gold, old, old, old, old, old…' Whisper fades as Narrator 1 speaks.

NARRATOR 1: The king was growing old, so old that wrinkles fell like waves down his face. Soon he would die. How should he divide his kingdom among his three daughters? He thought long about it and then came up with an answer.

KING: *[Stands]* I shall ask each one of my daughters who loves me the most! This is a very clever idea! *[He sits, looking pleased with himself]*

Servants and courtiers look up from their boredom

[Claps his hands] Come here, my faithful servants. Send news to all the lords, ladies and nobles that they must attend my most important, most ingenious ceremony this very afternoon. Go, make haste, prepare the room, and send for my daughters.

Music. Exaggerated hustle and bustle. Servants rush about frantically, making preparations, going out among the audience as though searching for nobles. The three daughters are led to stand before King

KING: Now, my oldest child, come forward and answer me this question, the same question that I shall ask of your two sisters. Think carefully, for your inheritance depends upon your reply.

Sisters 1 and 2 glance meaningfully at each other. Sister 1 makes an exaggerated and melodramatic curtsey

Daughter, *how* much do you love me?

SISTER 1: *[Aside, unheard by crowd or King]* His kingdom... my... our kingdom is at stake. I must take care to flatter an old man's pride. The reward is one most high! *[Changes her voice to a melodramatic, flattering tone and kneels at his feet]* Father, I love you more than all the jewels that encrust your fingers and all the gold that lies hidden down in the vaults of this castle! *[She stands and looks around in a self-satisfied way]*

KING: Indeed, indeed. *[Looks to all nobles for support – they anxiously copy his nodding]* A most pleasing answer. Now you, my middle daughter, what have you to say in reply to my question? Can you match your sister?

SISTER 2: *[She copies the exaggerated curtsey. Aside]* I must try hard. I shall not be outdone by *her*. Besides, I have my eye on Father's gold and jewels. *[She gives a little cough, kneels and then answers]* Father, I love you more than all the land of your kingdom that spreads like an ocean beyond this castle! *[She stands and looks around as though expecting applause]*

KING: Excellent, most excellent! These two answers please me greatly. Now come, youngest and dearest child of mine, tell us all, how do you love me?

NARRATOR 2: At last the younger daughter stepped forward, but stood her ground and did not bend her knee.

SALT PRINCESS: *[Aside]* I, who love my father most truly, must answer in an honest, down-to-earth way. I won't play the false games my sisters play. [*She turns back to answer*] Father, I love you more than... salt.

Simultaneous intake of breath from gathered crowd

KING: Salt? Salt! [*He shouts and stands*]

NARRATOR 3: The king was most in*salt*ed.

KING: *Thundering* salt is it? Hah! Well then, the day that salt becomes more precious than gold is the day you shall be my daughter once again! Leave this place in banishment, for you are no longer mine!

There is a shocked silence from everyone, then quiet murmuring. Courtiers 1 and 2 use a stage whisper to speak to each other

COURTIER 1: The king has spoken rashly as usual. Why does the old man never think before opening his mouth?

COURTIER 2: Yes, and of course his word is law, not to be broken by anyone. [*Gasps*] Look. There she goes...

Salt Princess walks forwards, staring straight ahead. Sisters 1 and 2 smile triumphantly at each other, then walk purposefully towards King and stand to one side behind him, looking as though plotting

SALT PRINCESS: [*Speaks as walking slowly*] Banished, banished, banished... Oh, my dear father, I shall love you forever, though your stubborn pride may never know it. Where... where shall I go...? Never to see these faces again?

All watch her go, craning forwards. As she finishes speaking, King and Sisters 1 and 2 turn to face back of stage

NARRATOR 4: So it was that the young princess left the castle with only the clothes she was wearing.

Cast make a forest for the Salt Princess to make her way through. Babichka moves forwards and stands with her back to the audience

NARRATOR 5: Surrounding the castle, for it was a long time

ago, a great forest spread into the horizon and soon the princess grew lost.

Salt Princess mimes fear and uncertainty as she trails through trees

NARRATOR 6: She was tired and her heart was so heavy. But then, as if in answer, a little path appeared in front of her. She followed it and the trees opened onto a clearing.

Path appears in the forest – cast step either side of a designated line

NARRATOR 7: In the middle stood a stone cottage, well kept and surrounded by vegetable gardens. The girl went to knock at the door.

Salt Princess knocks at door. Babichka answers by turning round to face her

BABICHKA: *[As though she has been waiting for her]* Ah, here you are. Welcome child. *[Holds out a piece of bread and sprinkles salt onto it, then offers it to Salt Princess, who takes it with a curtsey and takes a bite from it]* I am Babichka – old woman, grandmother. Some call me Wise One. What may I do for you?

SALT PRINCESS: I thank you for your gracious welcome. I need rest for the night and food, if you can help me, dear lady?

BABICHKA: You need more than rest, sweet child. *[Takes Salt Princess by hand]* But can you cook, sew, chop wood?

SALT PRINCESS: I can do none of these things, but I am willing to learn...

NARRATOR 1: And so the girl was welcomed into the little cottage and there she stayed, learning how to do things for herself, rather than waiting for them to be done for her.

Salt Princess and Babichka mime domestic activities

NARRATOR 2: The old woman was kind and soon the princess's heart settled down, though she never forgot her father, far away.

Salt Princess pauses, looks wistfully towards her father, then exits. Babichka sits down. Forest people turn to face King, resuming courtly stances. King and daughters turn back to face audience

Scene 9

NARRATOR 3: In the castle, the king was growing old. Now, he had only two daughters to choose from. Soon he would make his decision. And there must be a feast!

KING: *[Addressing servants]* A feast! Yes! Come on! *[He beckons the servants to join him immediately]* Are you noting this down? I want you to send word to my royal cook that we shall have the greatest feast ever prepared. I want all the kings, courtiers and important people of the realm here. No one shall forget the power of *my* kingdom.

SISTER 1: Oh yes, a simply wonderful idea, Father!

SISTER 2: You always have such clever ideas, Father.

They elbow each other, vying for attention. Improvise more false praise and flattery, as though trying to outdo each other in trying to get his attention

KING: *[To the servants, who have been watching the spectacle of the two daughters]* Come along, chop, chop!

Servants spring into action, rushing aimlessly around the stage to create an impression of chaos. Cook exits to put on hat and waistcoat. Kitchen staff sprawl at front and mime playing cards.

Babichka stands with her back to audience. King and Sisters 1 & 2 stay where they are, while the others form tableaux dotted around edge of stage as though they are staff around the castle, in the middle of doing something

NARRATOR 4: The day before the feast, there was a great thunderstorm, and it rained through day into night. Far away in the woods, Babichka smiled. The next morning, all *should* have been busy down in the cavernous kitchens. The cook was receiving orders.

Thunder sounds – pre-recorded or vocal. All react to the storm and rain. Spotlit, Babichka turns a full circle, on cue, smiling and nodding in a satisfied way then sits, back to audience. Cast remain in tableaux

Scene 10

Improvised scene. Kitchen staff are lazing around idly, playing cards and fooling around. Cook enters angrily. They jump up for an inspection of the cleanliness of their hands. Some are sent out to wash them. Cook tells them about the feast that has been requested and gives out the tasks. Comic business – fingers get sliced, food is burnt, crockery gets dropped – one of the characters can't do anything right and gets in everyone's way.

29

Scene 11

COOK: *[Takes out a pocket watch]* Aha! The time has come, my fellow feast-creators. I must visit the cellars for the royal stock of salt. Then the seasoning may begin. Let those flavours do a tap-dance on the taste buds! *[Exits]*

NARRATOR 5: Off went the cook, down the steps, when suddenly...

COOK: *[Screams offstage, then returns in a panic]* The king, the king, what will he say? What can be done? Oh my! *[Grabs own head as though holding it in place]* He'll surely chop off my head and stick it in a stew! I'm in a right pickle here! How am I going to tell him?

Kitchen staff improvise responses – 'What is it? Tell us! What can be that bad?' Cook then runs from one tableau group to another. He continues to run on the spot each time he stops, as does each immediate group as they, too, ask him questions. When he leaves each group, they reform into tableau position of running after him. Thus it creates impression that he's running all the way around the castle, with courtiers in pursuit, before he finally approaches King

COOK: *[Out of breath]* Oh most noble patron!

All look anxiously towards King

    Oh, how can I tell you? All the salt has been... washed away in the storm last night!

KING: WHAT? NO SALT? No salt in the royal cellars? Are you sure? Impossible!

All wince as though expecting a blow to fall

    [Changes mood] Ah, no matter. I am the king! I'll

simply send my fastest messengers to the four corners of the kingdom. *[He beckons the messengers]* They'll soon find salt. Wait here. *[He leans forward to whisper to the messengers, who then adopt a running position, each facing in a different direction]*

NARRATOR 6: But within the time it takes a heart to forget, the messengers returned with these words.

As they say lines, messengers swivel on spot to face King

MESSENGER 1: Your Majesty,

MESSENGER 2: what little salt there is

MESSENGER 3: is now more precious than gold.

MESSENGER 4: And none shall part with it.

An indrawn gasp from the onlookers

KING: What…?

NARRATOR 5: Then the king remembered what he had said to his daughter. But he was a king, and kings never show their feelings.

KING: So, cook of mine, make sweet dishes instead! Use sugar! Must I tell everyone how to do their job?

COOK: *[Muttering]* Sweet dishes? Sweet? Ridiculous! Whoever heard of sugar taking the place of salt? Still, he's the king. His sour-tongued word is law… *[He leaves, still muttering to himself]*

Scene 12

NARRATOR 6: So the nobles came, and their families, their servants, their baggage and horses.

Babichka exits. Cast divide into nobles and servants. Mime arrival. Long red sheet used to create long table, around which nobles stand, all holding sheet with one hand to pull it taut. Guards stand behind King, Sisters 1 and 2 on either side. Servants wait in readiness

NARRATOR 7: Slowly the feasting room filled. All was politeness, for the king was not a man to make an enemy of. *[Aside to audience, miming cut throat]* Trust me on this!

Improvise polite conversation among guests

KING: And now, my most welcome and noble friends, please be seated and let the feast begin.

Lower sheet slightly. Servants mime bringing food, pouring wine, etc

SISTER 1: A toast – the king!

ALL: The king!

Mimed glasses are raised for toast, set down and then nobles simultaneously lift forks and mime taking a bite. In sequence, one after the other, react with disgust and exaggerated facial expressions

NOBLES: *[Screeching to each other]* This is sweet!

They improvise descriptions of what they are tasting: 'Steak in custard!' 'Sausage and chocolate ice-cream' etc. They all lay down their forks simultaneously

NOBLE 1: I won't stand for being treated like this!

Nobles 1 and 2 rise to leave

NOBLE 2: Quite right! Is he trying to make fools of us?

Guests get up haughtily and leave in disgust, freezing at edges of the stage. King, guards, Sisters 1 and 2 and end table-holders remain

KING: What? How? What? All… gone? [*His pride gone, he slumps from upright posture, hangs his head and is finally helped offstage by two servants as Narrator 1 speaks*]

Cloth holders rapidly fold cloth and depart

NARRATOR 1: The great hall stood empty, apart from two smiling daughters who had no complaint about the food. The king's heart was so heavy, it could almost crack. And he would have cried, but tears have salt in them, so even they stayed stuck inside. Soon, he grew ill and had to be taken abed.

SISTER 1:   [*Smiling*] Well, sister, perhaps now we shall not have too long to wait.

SISTER 2:   [*Rubbing hands together*] Indeed, it can only be a matter of time. All that luvverly-jubberly gold!

SISTER 1:   And jewels and silver, mmmm!

SISTER 2:   And paintings and castles and… armies.

SISTER 1:   And power… Oooh, the thought of it makes my head go giddy!

Both giggle as they exit, heads together. Young Women 1 and 2 exit

Scene 13

Enter Babichka and Salt Princess.

NARRATOR 2: Far away in the forest, Babichka smiled also...

BABICHKA: It is time for you to make your way back home my lady! Your father is ill, and only you can help him. Take this. *[Hands her a small black bag]* It will help you on your journey. And when it is empty, remember to follow the wind over the three hills and through the three valleys. You will come to a grassy mound. Knock three times and you shall see what you shall see!

SALT PRINCESS: *[Takes bag and opens it and puts finger in]* It's... *[Licks finger]* salt! *[Looks questioningly at Babichka]* Thank you, Babichka, Wise One!

NARRATOR 2: Although she did not understand, the princess said nothing, but kissed the wise woman on both cheeks and left without looking back.

Cast spread out to make forest

The forest no longer filled her with fear, for she knew well its ways and wildness.

Exit Babichka. Salt Princess begins walking confidently but soon becomes lost and weary

NARRATOR 3: But for some reason, the way was longer and by the end of the day, the princess was once again lost and her heart grew heavy. As if in answer, a little path appeared in front of her. She followed it and the trees opened onto a clearing. Before her stood a poor-looking hovel.

Path appears and Salt Princess follows it to door formed by 2 performers. Young Woman 1 enters. She opens door, holding out a crust of bread

YOUNG WOMAN 1: I would welcome you in, my lady, but I have no salt for the bread. It was all washed away in the great storm!

SALT PRINCESS: *[To herself]* Now I understand. *[To Young Woman 1]* It is of no matter, I have salt here.

YOUNG WOMAN 1: Bless you, my lady. Will you rest with us this night? Come inside, it is late and dark. You are welcome to all we may offer.

Forest path closes around them as Salt Princess enters

NARRATOR 3: Day came again, as it always does, and the princess went on her way.

Forest parts and spreads out to let Salt Princess depart

But soon, she grew lost. She was tired and her heart was so heavy. Would she ever find her way home, and how would a bag of salt help her?

A path appears among trees

As if in answer, a little path appeared in front of her. She followed it and the trees opened onto a clearing. In the middle stood a fine merchant's house, made of good red brick.

She follows path to door. Young Woman 2 opens it, holding out piece of bread

YOUNG WOMAN 2: I would welcome you in, my lady, but I have no salt for the bread. It was all washed away in the great storm!

SALT PRINCESS: Of course. It is of no matter. I have salt, here.

YOUNG WOMAN 2: Bless you, my lady. Will you rest with us this night? Come inside, it is late and dark. You are welcome to all we may offer.

Salt Princess and Young Woman 2 move to rear of stage. Enter King and Sisters 1 and 2. All cast on stage move into new position. King is in bed. Physician and Guard 2 stand beside bed. 2 performers stand, shoulders together, between audience and King, representing curtains. 2 performers form palace gates front stage left with Guard 1 and Doorman either side. Sisters 1 and 2 stand at back. Rest of cast form crowd where Salt Princess entered merchant's house

Scene 14

NARRATOR 4: Day came once more, and with it word about the woman with salt had spread through the forest. Now a throng of folk stood outside the house.

Crowd mutters 'Who is she? Where has she come from?' Salt Princess and Young Woman 2 appear at edge of crowd

SALT PRINCESS: *[Leaving the house]* I thank you for your kindness and courtesy. Please take this as a token of my gratitude. Hold out your hands. *[Pours salt into hands]*

YOUNG WOMAN 2: My lady! Thank you!

SALT PRINCESS: *[Followed by crowd]* And now to the royal palace. Come, I shall lead the way. Who can give me news of the king?

Guard 1 stands in front of closed gates, doorman behind

CROWD LEADER: Have you not heard, lady? The king lies dying.

It is said that he is blind and calls only for his youngest daughter. Look, the castle gates are ahead. What shall you do?

Princess motions to the crowd to stand back and she steps forward

SALT PRINCESS: Guard! May I be permitted to try a cure for the king's blindness?

GUARD 1: Death is not far from the old man now. I'm sure you may try what you will. Here, doorman, escort the lady to see the king. She says she's got some sort of cure.

Doors open and close again quickly, blocking crowd who attempt to follow her. Crowd leader leads crowd, doors and Guard 1 to the back where they wait for news. Doorman leads Salt Princess to King

DOORMAN: Come my lady, to the cold room where the king lies.

Sisters notice what is happening and follow at a distance. They wait outside the door, listening. Doorman opens 'curtains'

NARRATOR 4: Curtains were drawn aside, and there lay the king, shrivelled up like a pea, his eyes gummed shut.

KING: Who is it? Who's there?

Physician and Guard 2 help King to his feet. He staggers and sinks to his knees.

PHYSICIAN: He is blind, lady. Even the salty tears of his eyes dried up, and without tears he cannot see.

In silence Salt Princess takes the last grains of salt and puts them on her lips. She then kisses King on both eyes

NARRATOR 5: And as she kissed each eyelid, the king began to cry a sea of tears.

KING: *[Hides head, then looks up]* Daughter, I see you! At last. Oh, daughter of mine, forgive me. *[Rises to feet]*

SALT PRINCESS: Father, my dear father!

KING: *[He holds her face in his hands]* My child. So like your mother. And I never saw… Do you remember when you were little, how I used to throw you in the air?

They laugh and embrace, then stand together in still tableau

Scene 15

Improvised scene. Sisters 1 and 2 vent their outrage, listening behind the door, showing how angry they are that she should return just now. How dare she ruin their plans? They are fearful that they will lose their inheritance. They both work themselves up to melodramatic hysteria, before running off stage cursing.

Scene 16

SALT PRINCESS: Now my bag of salt is empty. What was it Babichka told me? Father, I must leave you briefly, but this time I shall not be gone from your heart.

Cast form the hills and valleys described in the narration that follows, creating the landscape that the Salt Princess travels through and, eventually, the carriage that takes her back to the castle. Dance and gymnastics work well to create landscape and atmosphere

NARRATOR 5: And she ran with the wind out of the castle, past the crowd, over three hills and through three valleys until she came at last to a grassy mound. *[Formed by performers]* She knocked three times and the mound opened like a door.

NARRATOR 6: In front of her was a tunnel of ice, though it was not cold. *[Formed by performers and an unfurling long, white scarf]* She walked through and the tunnel grew into a cavern so deep, she could not see its end. In the middle stood a garden of white flowers. *[Performers, holding white paper flowers]* She bent to pluck one, and licked her fingers. It was made of… salt!

Salt Princess nods and smiles in realisation. Takes out her empty salt bag. Babichka enters at rear of stage. Stands with back to audience

NARRATOR 7: As understanding dawned, a white stallion appeared, drawing a fine white carriage fit for a queen.

Four performers using umbrellas suggest the wheels of a carriage. The performers stay still, twirling the wheels to show galloping. As an option a horse mask can also be used

NARRATOR 1: She got in and the horse galloped through the cavern, out of the tunnel, over three hills and down three valleys, until she arrived back within the castle courtyard.

Cast assemble in wonder and greeting around the carriage. Babichka is spotlit at back and turns to face audience

NARRATOR 2: Far away in the forest, Babichka smiled. There was a crack of thunder and horse, carriage, wheels, spokes and all dissolved into a mountain of salt on which sat the princess.

Large white sheet is pulled over carriage (umbrellas and performers).

Salt Princess is lifted behind mound to sitting height. King walks forwards in gesture of welcome and removes his crown. Salt Princess greets him and kneels before him. He places crown on her head

NARRATOR 3: Now the king would die happy and find peace.

King takes a step backwards, crosses his arms with hands resting on shoulders and drops head forwards

NARRATOR 4: As he closed his eyes, the salt turned into a glittering white throne.

NARRATOR 5: The princess was raised to her rightful place.

She is lifted in front of mound in shoulder-lift

NARRATOR 6: And hailed by all as

NARRATOR 7: the Queen of Salt.

All chant 'Salt! Salt! Salt'

Scene 17

Bards 1 and 2 barge on to finish the tale. Sisters 1 and 2 mime action described and cast observe and mime responses.

BARD 1:   Yeah! Yeah! That's all very nice.

BARD 2:   But what about her sisters? Did they pay the price?

BARD 1:   Truth is, they didn't believe in magic,

BARD 2:   and so their end, dear friends, was

BOTH: tragic!

BARD 1:   Take heed what happens when you mock:

BARD 2: on seeing such wonders, they both… died of shock!

Both sisters collapse and die in melodramatic fashion. Sister 1 refuses to die, and wriggles about. Bard 1 stalks over and hisses at her

BARD 1: You're supposed to be dead, not breathing. Pushing up daisies, popped yer clogs, kaput, dearly departed! Armpit scratching is not a usual occupation for the recently deceased. Get it?

Both finally lie still

BARD 1: *[Checks for signs of life by prodding with toe]* OK. That's better. Job done. *[Pause]* You can get up now. And the rest of you. Yes, that's it, go on, off you go. Ta ra for now.

Cast exit

BARD 2: *[Sighs]* Just can't get the professionals! Where was I? Ah yes… they died of shock.

BOTH: Awwww!

BARD 1: Can't say it's all that sad,

BARD 2: I mean, look at the way they treated their dad!

Aside to each other

BARD 2: You could almost say… wait for it… Revenge is… *sweet*-er than gold!

BARD 1: *[Deadpan]* Is that another attempt at humour?

BARD 2: *[Insulted]* Of course! Today… *[insert place of performance, town, school etc]*, tomorrow: my own comic series.

BARD 1: Yeah. Right. Excuse my friend. He needs a dose of sanity! *[Hits Bard 2 over head with prop of choice – could be big salt-grinder]*

BARD 2: Owww! I'm sick of being stuck inside this rhyme!

BARD 1:   Tough! Listen, we're nearly out of time

BARD 2:   for our last tale with a twist, so sit, take note.

BARD 1: This one's called *Nasrudin's Coat*.

BARD 2: Nasrudin: trickster, clever fool,

BARD 1: quick-witted master of misrule.

BARD 2: An underdog with attitude.

BARD 1: His jokes are wise, his antics rude.

BARD 2: This legend, passed from ancient East

BARD 1: asks, 'Who's the fool by the final feast?'

Exit

NASRUDIN'S COAT: AN ANCIENT PERSIAN TALE

Scene 18

Cast enter (minus Nasrudin), carrying chairs to use in tableaux and in feasting scene. They arrange themselves in groups around the stage. As each narrator speaks, the groups switch into tableaux that represent each word or description.

NARRATOR 1: Tricks!

Cast adopt tableaux and facial expressions depicting trickery

NARRATOR 2: Tomfoolery!

Cast adopt tableaux of fooling about

NARRATOR 3: Plain stupidity.

Cast adopt tableaux

NARRATOR 4: So many faces Nasrudin wears.

Cast turn to audience. Each adopts facial expression from previous 3 descriptions. Facial expressions are then changed as narrators speak to demonstrate each of the following descriptions

NARRATOR 5: From prankster…

Cast depict laughing jokers with faces

NARRATOR 6: to con-artist. Fool…

Faces show deliberate plotting then depict vacant-looking fools

NARRATOR 7: to philosopher. Keeper of mystic wisdom.

Faces show deep thought. Then cast smile and cross arms in synchronised motion as though hiding something

NARRATOR 1: Which face will he wear for this tale?

All drop heads forward and adopt neutral expression. Nasrudin enters, looking weary. Groups adopt family tableaux. Aunt and servants adopt haughty tableau, slightly apart from others

> Well now, on this day, Nasrudin had been travelling for a long, long time.

Nasrudin mimes tiredly walking from group to group, but doesn't visit Aunt

NARRATOR 2: Through desert and village, from mosque to hovel, visiting his many relatives.

As he waves farewell to last group, the groups reform into a different sequence of proud and arrogant-looking nobles

NARRATOR 3: He was tired, dusty and weary and had but one relative left to see: a distant aunt, a widow whose husband had left her in a very rich and prosperous position.

Aunt is seated, looking haughty, with servants in attendance. Other groups turn and look towards her

NARRATOR 4: And this aunt was famous throughout the region, not only for her wealth but for her lavish parties, and, in particular, for her most delicious feasts.

NARRATOR 5: Of course, only the most noble of the noble were invited.

Group of nobles look down noses at audience

> But all who came could look forward to a dish whose reputation had travelled far and wide.

NARRATOR 6: Couscous! A salad of bulgar wheat and crunchy vegetables. But not *any* old couscous. Oh no – this was couscous made from Auntie's own wheat and from vegetables grown in no less than the emperor's very own gardens.

As Narrator 7 says following lines a performer from one of groups of nobles steps out of group, pulls chef's hat from belt and puts it on. Mimes carrying a huge platter to Aunt. Nobles mime clapping

NARRATOR 7: And as if this wasn't enough, she hired the most famous cook in all the land to prepare each feast. No wonder the fame of her food had spread.

Cook bows, removes hat and returns to group

NARRATOR 1: And no wonder she had so many eager guests.

Groups vie with each other. Wave and try to catch Aunt's attention

Why, an invitation to one of her gatherings was an honour indeed.

NARRATOR 2: Nasrudin was hungry and thirsty.

Nasrudin mimes

Just two more hours of the heat and the dust and he'd be there!

Cast move into banqueting positions. Servant moves centre front and two cast members form doors in front of servant. Music covers movement on stage

NASRUDIN: Oh, how my poor, parched mouth would water, if only it could. Oh, the vision of the food I shall taste! And a bath and cool sheets... nearly there now... let me see... ah yes, the carved doors, how could I forget? Oh, my stomach is shrivelled as a dry pea-pod! [*Clutches stomach as though rumbling. Steps forward and mimes knocking*]

SERVANT: [*Opens doors. Looks at Nasrudin suspiciously*] What do you want, beggar? How dare you knock here? Off

45

with you – impudent wretch, back to the gutter where you belong! *[Servant turns, and with a flourish, pulls out a white duster and polishes the spot where Nasrudin knocked – probably one of the door's noses]*

NASRUDIN: *[Taps Servant on shoulder – Servant turns furiously and wipes shoulder with cloth]* Er, but I am Nasrudin. I am here to visit my esteemed aunt!

SERVANT: Your aunt? Are you sure? Are you QUITE sure? At THIS house?

NASRUDIN: Yes. I am. And I'm sure she wouldn't be happy to hear I'd been kept waiting in the street.

SERVANT: Hmmm. If you say so. You'd better come in. But DON'T touch anything. And don't breathe so close to me. *[Leads Nasrudin offstage]*

Scene 19

Music. Guests mime feasting. Nasrudin is led back onstage.

NARRATOR 3: And so Nasrudin was led along cool, marble corridors, past tinkling fountains, beautiful rugs and lavish silk drapes until, at last, he could hear the sounds of people feasting. He had reached the banqueting hall – and what a sight!

Sounds of laughter and shrill voices. Music continues as Nasrudin looks around with his mouth open. Music fades

SERVANT: As you can see, your visit is, ah, unexpected, so I won't disturb the mistress now. She's busy. This way.

As he leads Nasrudin past the guests, they turn up their noses in mock disgust and shriek to each other in ever more shrill voices

> Here! *[He motions to very edge of stage and places a battered-looking table in front of Nasrudin. On this he unceremoniously dumps a plate and a chipped mug]* Some leftovers. I'm sure you'd find the guests' banquet far too rich for your constitution.

Nasrudin hands his hat to Servant who looks alarmed and immediately throws it away. Servant moves away to attend to guests

NASRUDIN: Well! What a welcome! Still, it's food. *[Sniffs it]* I think. And at least I can wash the dust down. *[Takes a mouthful of drink and spits it out again. Speaks hoarsely]* Or perhaps not. But it's cool here and pleasant. I'll enjoy the surroundings, and the 'entertainment'. *[Watches for a while then falls asleep with head slumped forwards]*

Music. There is background noise of chatting and eating

GUEST 1: Yes, marvellous occasion isn't it?

GUEST 2: Of course, anyone who is anyone is here tonight. Have you seen the emperor's daughter? Perfectly dreadful jewels she's wearing but still, worth an absolute fortune!

Polite laughter

GUEST 3: Superb food. I say, any more wine anywhere? It's vintage stuff this. Thought I might try and smuggle out a couple of flagons.

GUEST 4: Our hostess is looking well isn't she?

GUEST 5: For her age.

GUEST 4: Has she made her will yet? Anyone know?

GUEST 5: No children.

GUEST 4: Just her devoted friends.

GUEST 5: And relations of course. I suppose she must have relatives?

GUEST 4: Pah! What are relatives, compared with dear friends such as ourselves?

GUEST 5: You are so right. We really must make sure she knows how 'dear' she is to us, mustn't we?

GUEST 4: Indeed...

GUEST 6: Sssshh, don't look, she's coming our way. Have you SEEN what she's got round her neck?

GUEST 7: SO vulgar. You'd think she'd have more refined taste really, wouldn't you?

Aunt arrives next to them

Ah! Our gallant and elegant hostess. And SUCH an unusual creation. *[Points to necklace]* You simply MUST tell me where you commissioned it. It's splendid! Look everyone! Do!

Aunt shows off her necklace. There is gentle and polite applause

GUEST 1: Wonderful feast, as always. I hear you're having another one tomorrow. Has my invitation been... delayed... perhaps?

AUNT: *[Coughs a little nervously]* You are always welcome. You don't need the formality of an invitation!

Everyone looks up at her very expectantly

You are ALL always welcome of course!

There is polite laughter and murmurs of 'We knew that,' and 'How nice,' and 'The mark of a truly dear friend!'

So, until tomorrow my friends. I am most pleased you

enjoyed the feast and I wish you all a pleasant night's sleep. I shall be retiring soon myself. Farewell.

GUEST 2: Quite so, quite so. Come along everyone, gather yourselves.

Cast exit to sides, improvising goodnight conversations. As they pass Nasrudin they stick their noses in the air and mutter to each other about how disgraceful it is that he should be lowering the tone of the evening. Nasrudin sleeps on, oblivious, until only he, Aunt and Servant are left

AUNT: *[Yawns]* Another excellent evening. The emperor's daughter was MOST impressed with the food. She's promised to come again soon and to bring some of her most influential friends. A triumph! A great success! A… who on EARTH is that? *[Sees Nasrudin]*

SERVANT: He claims to be your nephew, Mistress. He arrived earlier with this tale and was quite adamant he was related to you. Shall I have the impostor removed?

AUNT: Yes! Right away! The very idea! *[Turns then hesitates]* Did he give a name?

SERVANT: *[Thinks]* Rudenose-in… Noseraggin… Nasrudin, something like that. False, no doubt…

AUNT: *[Looks ill]* Oh dear. I'm mortified to say that it's possible he could be a relative. Oh. How distasteful. Yes, I think he does resemble one of my sister's numerous offspring, though of course, it's many years since… Wake him up would you?

Servant kicks Nasrudin who wakes with a start

NASRUDIN: Wha…? Ah, my noble aunt, how nice of you to greet me so courteously. It's such a long time since we met. There must be so many questions you wish to ask me.

AUNT: What are you doing here? What do you want? *[To Servant]* What was his name again?

NASRUDIN: Want? Why, to visit the sister of my dear mother.

AUNT: Hmmmmmmm. How nice. *[Sniffs with a look of disgust]* Have you taken a bath recently?

NASRUDIN: Why, how kind of you to offer! I can't remember the last time I had the chance. That's just what I've been longing for. Perhaps your servant could show me the way?

AUNT: Oh… NO! No, quite out of the question I'm afraid, ah, there's a… a… shortage of water. Yes! That's it! No water. And of course, I would ask you to stay the night, but as you can see, this is a humble abode and there are just not quite enough rooms.

NASRUDIN: *[Looks around with raised eyebrows]* Really? How surprising. I passed so many doors on my way in!

AUNT: Yes! Um… Decorating! Being decorated – refurnished, new wall hangings. Terrible mess! Couldn't possibly expect you to put up with the… inconvenience. No, no indeed. I'm sure you'll find somewhere much more to your liking in the town. In fact, you'd better get going now while there's still time. *[To Servant]* Show him out through the back courtyard will you?

NASRUDIN: Right! Well, lovely to see you looking so well Aunt. *[Holds out his hand]*

AUNT: *[Ignores his hand]* Mmm?? Oh, yes, charming to see you again too after all this time, and looking so… so… *[She looks him up and down]* so… Yes, quite so. Have a good journey home won't you. Goodnight.

NASRUDIN: *[Bows, a little too close to her. She jumps back]* Until we meet again. *[Exits]*

AUNT: I sincerely hope not. What a gruesome ending to such a splendid evening. *[She exits]*

Enter Nasrudin and narrators. Nasrudin mimes actions described

NARRATOR 4: And so Nasrudin found himself outside once more. But he was not a man to worry and off he went, confident that the night would give him somewhere to sleep.

NARRATOR 5: And behold, just as he left the house, the moon glinted with a lady-luck smile. He looked closer in the dusty shadows and there! A fine gold coin! His for the taking.

Nasrudin bites the coin

NARRATOR 6: Perfect! A rare one too – worth a great deal. Now that would come in handy. Nasrudin skipped off happily and found his way to a comfortable guesthouse where he fell into a soft and silent sleep. *[Exits]*

Scene 20

Brief blackout – then lights up, indicating bright day. Cast enter. Seven members of cast move into line for next section. Each one mimes each separate action (serving, polishing, hairdressing etc) described by Narrator 7. Visually, it is as though Nasrudin is being passed down a conveyer-belt of people. Rest of cast mime being market traders/shoppers etc. Tailor enters.

NARRATOR 7: The next day, Nasrudin had a few preparations to make. First he ate a hearty breakfast, settled his bill, and set off to have his hair oiled and perfumed. A close shave followed. Then he bought a pair of shoes from a market trader, paused to have them polished, and stopped to admire his reflection in a glass door.

Another cast member mimes being mirrored reflection

Better! But not quite complete. Not yet... Finally, he found his way to a tailor's shop.

Cast move into frozen street scene. Nasrudin and Tailor mime the actions described

Measurements were taken, patterns discussed and haggling over price conducted.

Tailor and Nasrudin shake hands

It was agreed that Nasrudin should return before sundown.

Nasrudin walks to side of stage. All freeze. Lights indicate late afternoon/sunset. Chiming of bell. Nasrudin comes to life. Rest of cast stay frozen

NASRUDIN: Is it ready?

TAILOR: It is indeed. Step this way. I have been hard at work
          all day. The finest cloth – as requested. The best cut,
          the most delicate stitching. And of course, all the
          grandest details. It's a beauty, though I say so myself.
          Ah! Here we are. *[Unwraps coat from tissue paper and
          shakes it out]* There! *[He holds it out to Nasrudin. Coat
          is extremely opulent]*

NASRUDIN: PERFECT! Just exactly what I had in mind. *[Tries it
          on]* Yes! An excellent job – worth every last coin of
          my lucky find. Thank you a thousand times over.
          Here is your payment *[Hands over a small bag of coins]*
          I shall enjoy this coat VERY much.

TAILOR: Thank *you* kind sir. I wish you a long and prosperous
          life and a most pleasant evening ahead. *[Bows]*

NASRUDIN: Indeed. *[Exits, grinning broadly]*

Music plays

Scene 21

*Street scene. Cast can perform any skills that can be incorporated
into a street performance scene, eg acrobatics, gymnastics, juggling,
belly dancing, musical busking. Nasrudin observes for a while and
gives money before moving off. Cast form crowds that Nasrudin
passes through. As he passes they turn to look and comment.
Nasrudin walks as though following streets, with head held high. He
arrives in front of doors (formed by cast members) once more.
Servant is behind doors, as before.*

Scene 22

NASRUDIN: Here we are again. *[He pats down his hair and rubs his shoes behind each leg to polish them. Knocks – Servant opens doors]* Good evening.

SERVANT: *[Smiling and bowing]* Why, good evening to you, good sir. *[Looks Nasrudin up and down appreciatively]* No need to present your invitation, I can see that you are a guest of the highest distinction. Please, step this way.

NASRUDIN: Indeed, I am a distant relative of the lady of the house.

SERVANT: Marvellous! Then you've arrived just in time. There's a great feast about to begin and I'm certain my lady would wish you to be treated as a guest of honour. Please follow me. *[Closes doors]*

Music as cast form into guest groups around tables. Servant leads Nasrudin around and behind the stage, re-entering from other side

You must, of course, have the best seat. This way if you please.

Nasrudin bows to the guests as he passes and stops to mime polite conversation

GUEST 8: I say, who's that fellow? Do we know him?

GUEST 9: If we don't, we certainly ought to.

GUEST 10: Good gracious yes. What a fine figure he cuts! Has anyone here had the pleasure of his acquaintance?

GUEST 11: Not me, I'm afraid, though I shall change that as soon as possible. He looks jolly important.

GUEST 12: Mmmmm, yes, influential, distinguished...

GUEST 13: And wealthy – he MUST be rich, just look at him.

GUEST 14: No doubt about it: LOADED! Where's he sitting?

GUEST 8: Oh I say! Next to the hostess herself.

GUEST 12: Do you think he could be royal?

GUEST 9: Ssshh – I'm trying to hear what they're saying.

Nasrudin and Servant have arrived at Aunt's table. Servant makes a great show of getting Nasrudin seated with a flourish

AUNT: Good evening sir! And welcome to my humble gathering. It's marvellous to see that such a noble friend is willing to grace me with his presence. *[Aside, to Servant]* Remind me who this fine gentleman is.

SERVANT: A relative of yours – just arrived.

AUNT: Indeed, my kinsman! I am most honoured by your visit. In fact, you must be the first to taste the banquet tonight. *[To Servant]* Bring forth the special dish. *[To Nasrudin]* I DO hope it will be to your liking. My friends seem to enjoy it.

A plate of couscous is brought out and placed before Nasrudin

More wine for my guests, while my noble friend here does me the honour of tasting the first plate of my modest offering.

Mime pouring of wine and raising of glasses while Nasrudin prepares himself to eat

Do start.

NASRUDIN: I am most grateful to my elegant hostess and kinswoman. Now then. *[He turns to the plate and, with a big show, scoops up some of the couscous with a spoon.*

*He raises it towards his mouth, but at the last moment,
wipes it down his coat and smears it around with his
other hand]*

*Aunt gasps and slowly all the guests start to put down their mimed
glasses, stop murmuring and watch. Nasrudin puts down the spoon
and picks up handfuls of the couscous, rubbing it into his coat and
under his armpits*

NASRUDIN: *[Whispers at first, then grows louder until shouting]*
How does it taste? How does it taste? Is it good? Are
you enjoying it? How does it taste? Is it nice? How
does it taste? How many flavours? Is it delicious?

AUNT: *[Interjects]* Please… what… I say… please… stop…
everyone's looking…

When Nasrudin stops and turns to look at her, she speaks again

What? Pray, WHAT is the meaning of this
behaviour?

NASRUDIN: *[Looking innocent]* Sorry? Is there something wrong?
Ooh, missed a bit. *[He makes to take another handful
but she stops him]*

AUNT: Stop! Tell me! WHY are you doing this?

NASRUDIN: What? *[Again, looks blank then pretends to
understand]* Oh, I see, you mean the food? *[Looks
perplexed]* But I assumed that was what you expected.
Oh dear, have I made a mistake? *[He smiles]*

AUNT: What are you talking about?

NASRUDIN: Simple! You see, yesterday when I, your nephew,
arrived at your house in my usual travelling clothes
and my favourite hat, I was led to the lowest of the
low tables and given stale leftovers and sour beer.

AUNT: *[To Servant]* What's he going on about? *[She gives a nervous laugh]*

NASRUDIN: And then, of course, I was thrown out. Not welcome in your beautiful home!

AUNT: Well...

NASRUDIN: But today, when I, your nephew Nasrudin, arrived at your house in my fine new coat, I was led to the highest of the high tables to sit at your side. I was given the freshest couscous on a silver platter, with the most pleasing wine to drink.

AUNT: But I don't...

NASRUDIN: Now, as I, Nasrudin, am the same person as I was yesterday, then it's absolutely clear... I can only conclude that it cannot be ME you invited to dine with you this evening, but... MY COAT!

There is a shocked silence as everyone turns away guiltily. Blackout. All stay frozen. Bards 1 and 2 move to front of stage. Lights up

Scene 23

BARD 2: *[Doesn't get it]* What a weirdo! Trying to feed his coat!

BARD 1: *[To audience]* Excuse me while I get my hands round his throat! *[Tries to strangle Bard 2]*

BARD 2: *[Struggles valiantly, cries of 'Leave it out. I can't breathe!' etc]* But that classy kit cost loads of money.

BARD 1: You **still** don't get it? It's supposed to be funny! *[Head in hands with despair]*

BARD 2: *[Continues regardless]* I'll give him this… that Nasrudin's plucky.

BARD 1: Oh, I give up. Third time lucky. *[Hits Bard 2 over head with appropriate prop – maybe rubber chicken]* Can we finish now? These three tales, in their own way,

BARD 2: reveal that pride has come to stay. Dumb and blind to that which lies

BARD 1: like a jewel before their eyes.

BARD 2: Finally, they'll pay the price

BARD 1: not once, not twice, but three times thrice. *[Aside to audience]* You see – it all happens in threes. Three stories: beginning, middle and end and three clobbers over the head. Spooky coincidence huh?

BARD 2: Two daughters' greed; stepmother's pride.

BARD 1: A welcome, judged on looks, denied.

BARD 2: Some do not learn at legend's school.

BARD 1: Unseeing, each ends up the fool. *[Aside to audience, pointing at Bard 2]* Him too!

BARD 2: And victims that were once laid low

BARD 1: can dance and sing, 'I told you so!'

BARD 2: When upside down is flipside up

BARD 1: at last we'll drink from wisdom's cup. *[Raises imaginary cup. Bard 2 tries to steal it]*

BARD 2: And all you merry ones, take heed:

BOTH: be ruled by love, not wanton greed!

THE END

Set, prop and costume suggestions

In order to keep transitions between scenes as smooth and unobtrusive as possible, the set is, ideally, dictated by what can remain on stage throughout the performance. Stage blocks are useful for differentiated height and to denote different areas of action, using lighting.

Fabric can also be used to suggest different settings. The king's throne in *Salt is Sweeter than Gold* can be suggested using purple fabric over a stage block, and the salt cavern and mound using white scarves or floaty material. A length of cloth can be stretched and held at table height to form the banqueting table in *Salt is Sweeter than Gold,* and smaller pieces of cloth can be held taut by groups to form individual feasting tables in *Nasrudin's Coat.* A small, lightweight table and chair (preferably child-size, for reduced status) is required for Nasrudin to sit at alone for his first arrival at his aunt's house.

For themed links in choices about set, costume and music for performance – anything goes! The timeless nature of the tales themselves makes them ideally suited to being set in specific historic or cultural locations from 1920s decadence, 1960s psychedelia, 70s punk, Eastern European folk to Bollywood. Sharp, contemporary links can be drawn through the contrast of the traditional language used with up-to-date visual and musical references.

THE TWELVE STONES

Stepmother and Stepsister – wear high-status, luxurious fabrics or, for a contemporary twist, designer labels. Stepmother needs a small, metal box.

Evichka – threadbare and ragged clothes. She carries a basket.

The Twelve Stones – hooded capes. Hoods up when stones face away from audience and pushed back when stones turn and transform into men. Half-face masks are effective, particularly for the four seasons:

Old Man Winter – white beard.

Spring – wears green, with leaves. Carries an axe.

Summer – wears gold, flowers. Box of glitter/confetti with lid.

Autumn – wears brown/red/orange leaves.

Fire dancers – scarves or capes. Half-face masks also effective. Need fabric violets and strawberries, and apples.

SALT IS SWEETER THAN GOLD

King – crown.

Salt Princess – white cloak when changes into Queen of Salt.

Cook – chef's hat.

Babichka – black/grey cloak and wooden staff. Bag of salt.

White paper flowers.

NASRUDIN'S COAT

Two costumes for Nasrudin: 1) Scruffy, including battered hat
                            2) Opulent coat

Aunt – height of luxurious fashion. Large necklace.

Servant – pristine, white clothing. Duster in pocket.

Tailor – fitted suit.

Guests – glamorous finery. Chef's hat for scene 18.

Gold coin.

Plate of couscous on silver platter.

Rehearsal and Workshop ideas

Ways in

Pool Table: As the whole cast remains on stage for much of the action of these stories, it is vital that all performers should be able to maintain a strong group focus. This exercise is useful for developing and then commenting on the sensory and spatial awareness of a whole group.

Imagine that the rehearsal space is one huge pool table. Each performer is like a billiard ball, moving slowly in a straight line, diagonally across the space until the edge is reached and the ball rebounds and moves in a different trajectory. Collision is not allowed! In order to avoid contact, a small step to one side may be made before continuing in the line of focus.

Initially a leader shouts instructions to stop and start. Everyone must obey immediately, in unison and stay in frozen position until instructed to move again. Instructions are also given to speed up and slow down. The aim is for the group to keep to the same pace.

After a while, continue the exercise with no leader giving instructions. The group still stops and starts, speeds up and slows down. This means that everyone has to develop a sort of extra-sensory group awareness, as the aim is for everyone to stop and start simultaneously, without any one leader emerging. Keep running the exercise in absolute silence and ask individuals to step out for a few moments each to observe the rest of the group, before rejoining. When finished, share observations: how it felt, what it looked like from the outside.

Wood You Believe It? The first two stories in the trilogy require the cast to physically suggest location and atmosphere by representing forests and a fire. In pairs and individually, create gnarled tree shapes. Move everyone closer together so that the forest appears more tangled. Choose an individual to get lost or trapped in the forest. Branches move and bar the way or open to reveal a path.

Try out the next exercise, Walk This Way (below), then mix the two exercises together. Begin by walking in any of the ways suggested. A leader shouts 'change.' Everyone instantly adopts forest formation and freezes in position. Repeat until forest transformation is instant.

Walk This Way: This is a whole-group, warming up exercise to help develop role and character. Everyone moves around the rehearsal space in the following manners:

Shy	Fearful
Over the moon/joyful	Furious/angry
Sly/plotting	Tired
Sad	Proud/superior
Cheerful/friendly	Suspicious/mean-spirited

As a variation, freeze the movement. Everyone freezes in a still statue that represents the mood or characteristic they have been walking with.

How Do You Do? Move around the space greeting each other formally (by shaking hands) in:

Proud/snobbish manner	Humble manner
Cheerful/friendly manner	Slobbish manner

Divide into 4 groups, allocating one manner to each group. Repeat exercise but now also respond to how the other person is greeting you. For example, a proud person will look down their nose at any of the other three. Humble may be taken aback by cheerful or slob. Slob will find snob either amusing or offensive, or will be oblivious etc. These caricatures are useful for introductory work on some of the main characters in the three tales.

There are a number of stage directions throughout *Flipside* for using tableaux (frozen pictures) to show fragments of action. Read any one of the scripted tales, each person delivering the next line. In pairs or small groups, prepare a snapshot (tableau) of one moment from the story. Show each in turn and invite comment on which part it shows, where the central point of focus is in each picture and anything else that makes it effective, such as: use of different heights, facial expression, posture etc.

Add in the moment before and the moment after to create three linked tableaux.

More group tableaux: Pick scenes, moments of action or themes from any of the tales and use tableaux to represent them. Themes: conspiracy, greed/selfishness, forgiveness, pride, reconciliation, wisdom, the dawning of realisation/truth, determination.

Vocal sound effects are required for *The Twelve Stones*. Experiment with ways of creating a specific atmosphere using layered voices in choral effect.

Begin by using the word 'lost'. The group repeats the word in a loud whisper, first with a short vowel sound on the 'o' and then with a long, drawn-out sound. Alter volume and pitch. How can the atmosphere be made first threatening and then dreamy by changing the delivery of the repeated word? Move on to making a range of cold sounds - shivering, shushing, whooshing and creaking.

Divide the group in half. One half repeats 'lost', the other layers cold sounds over the top of the lost chant. Raise and lower volume. Vary speed of delivery. Comment on the effect on an audience.

Human Props: At various points in the three plays, stage directions are given for performers to physically form parts of the set, props or locations, eg fire in a fireplace, opening doors, gates, small hill with doorway, horse-drawn carriage. In small groups, devise shapes and structures – static and moving, using the list above.

There are servants' roles in both *Salt is Sweeter than Gold* and *Nasrudin's Coat*. As a focusing exercise for individuals within a large group, everyone mimes carrying a tray of full glasses, balanced on one hand. Begin by clearly visualising the tray and the glasses. Try holding something such as a school or kit bag on one hand and observe how your arm muscles take the weight.

Return to mime: hold balancing-hand up at shoulder height. Everyone moves around each other as though serving very fast at a banquet. No collisions are allowed and concentration must be maintained on the tray, even when moving quickly. Aim to move the whole body in balance with the imagined tray.

Ask everyone to freeze, and allocate one or two individuals to keep moving around the frozen statues while everyone observes them for the authenticity of their movements.

Status

In all three stories, the characters that believe and act as though they have the highest status have their status levels reversed by the end. Seeing characters that are self-obsessed, conceited, arrogant and pompous undergo serious comeuppances and ego deflation is satisfying for the audience. There is a lot of interplay between characters using the traditional structure of master and servant or high and low social status levels.

1. In a large circle, introduce yourself to the rest of the group by stepping forward and saying, 'Hello. My name is…' For the first round, do this while adopting the mannerisms and delivery of someone of very high status. Consider which words are emphasised and how. Ensure that posture, body-language and gesture convey status as much as vocal delivery.

   For the second round, adopt the mannerisms and body language of someone with very low status (for the purpose of the exercise, think slob).

   Comment on how status was effectively (or indeed humorously) conveyed.

2. In pairs, 'sculpt' each other into a statue of 'snooty royalty'. Think about posture and body language as above. Statues hold their position while all sculptors move around to look at other statues. Comment on how individual stances suggest or reveal status. Swap round and repeat.

3. Everyone adopts the royal, snooty statue pose from above. Bring the statue to life as a character by experimenting with the most appropriate way of:
   a) walking
   b) sitting down
   c) eating

   Choose some individual characterisations to observe as a group and comment on how status is being physically conveyed.

4. Use the snooty characters from exercise 3 above – but drop the royal element – for an imperious and very self-important character. In small groups, improvise introductions at an extremely high-status function or party. Everyone tries to outdo everyone else in terms of self-importance. Everyone is aiming to make an impression regarding power/influence.

5. Repeat exercises 2 and 3 above, but for the low-status (or slob) character from the introductory exercise.

6. In pairs, each person adopts either high or low status. Repeat exercise 1. The high-status character should reveal their disgust physically as well as in the subtext of what is said. The low-status character should seem oblivious to the difference in status. This exercise is particularly relevant for the third tale, *Nasrudin's Coat.*

Character Development

Nasrudin's Coat: As an introductory-character building exercise, everyone walks around the space as
> a) Nasrudin, tired, thirsty and hot (at the beginning
of the tale)
>> b) Aunt, moving among guests, waving and air-kissing
>> c) Servant, as though leading Nasrudin, looking down nose at him.

Salt Princess and Evichka: The youngest daughter in *Salt is Sweeter than Gold*, and Evichka in *The Twelve Stones* share certain characteristics. They are both subservient to the will of their parent/step-parent. However, both maintain a calm, inner dignity and stand in contrast to the other apparently high-status characters. They both demonstrate a nobility that is lacking in others. Theirs is a very subtle form of attitude: a strength and grace of character that shows up those around them.

For the performers playing these roles, it is important to strike a balance between carrying out orders without complaint or question, whilst demonstrating inner spirit. This will be revealed in demeanour: posture, facial expression and the way that hands and shoulders are held. In pairs, devise a 'master and servant' routine. The master makes ever more outrageous demands. The servant complies.

Perform the same, basic routine in two different ways. Firstly, the servant should be deeply servile, almost squirming. Mannerisms should be fluttering and nervous, speech should be hesitant, breathy and slightly high-pitched, and posture should be lowly: curved shoulders, bowed spine and small, bobbing movements of the head.

Before repeating for the second version, servant should take a moment to undertake a breathing exercise: stand with feet shoulder-width apart, spine comfortably straight, shoulders relaxed and hands loosely by sides with palms flat. Look straight ahead, tipping head neither forwards nor backwards, but keeping it comfortably balanced. Breathe slowly and deeply. After a few moments, place hands just below rib cage. Keep shoulders very relaxed. Imagine that each breath is being drawn up from the ground beneath your feet, up under your ribs. When breathing out, imagine the breath sinking back down into the ground, rooting you to the spot.

Repeat the improvisation. This time, servant responds to orders as before, but alters body language. Shoulders are straight, but not tense. Eyes are lowered, but not head. Arms are relaxed and hand movements kept to a minimum. All movements are at an even pace and speech is calmly delivered and clearly enunciated. After a while, experiment with making occasional eye contact with master. What is the effect of this?

In groups, observe these two routines and comment on the differences in attitude and character of the servant suggested by each one.

As the whole cast for each tale spends much of the time on stage, everyone needs to maintain a strong focus of attention on the action. Events on stage need an ensemble response, in role. Place two chairs on stage. Assembled cast responds to the chairs with facial expression and body language as though the chairs are performers! Respond as though the action being observed is:

Shocking	Amusing
Annoying	Thought-provoking
Exciting	Sad
Boring	Surprising

TWISTED

Gretel is a fairly average teen: she falls out with her dad and has issues with her boyfriend. But in one way Gretel is different – she is in a coma. How did she get there? In this tale full of twists and turns there is more than one suspect...

KICK OFF

Enter the football-crazy world of Diddlebury Heights: a hypochondriac coach, a pompous headmaster, rapping cheerleaders, a stolen trophy and commentators with puns more disgraceful than the team's pitiful performance. Will the school be saved from the evil developer who has her eye on the very land it is built on?

MUCH ADO ABOUT CLUBBiNG

Saturday night will never be seen in the same way again! *Much Ado about Clubbing* is packed with cheesy chat up lines, girls with attitude, wannabe Romeos, awkward teenagers, and comedy double-act bouncers.